Sparrow's Lesson

Retold by Jill McDougall
from an Indian fable

Illustrations by Valerie Valdivia

Crow and Sparrow were good friends.

One day, they were hopping along the ground together when Crow picked up something small and shiny.

"What did you find, Crow?" asked Sparrow.

Crow put the small, shiny thing underneath his wing.
"It's nothing important," he said.

"Show it to me anyway!" cried Sparrow.

"It's nothing important!" said Crow again.

And he flew up into a tree.

Sparrow stared at Crow. She felt cross.

"What a bad bird you are!" she said, loudly. "I don't want to be your friend any more!"

Then, Sparrow hopped into the barn where Old Pony was eating hay.

“Hello, Old Pony,” said Sparrow.
“I’m feeling quite annoyed with Crow!
He won’t show me what he found!”

Old Pony wanted to finish eating his hay, so he turned his back and kept eating.

This made Sparrow *really* cross!

Sparrow's friend Mouse was sitting near the hay.

"Hello, Mouse," said Sparrow.
"Old Pony won't talk to me!
Please leap onto his tail and chew it!"

Mouse looked surprised.
"I don't want to chew Old Pony's tail,"
she said. "Why should I?"

Now Sparrow was annoyed with Mouse!

She hopped over to Cat, and said,
"Cat! I want you to frighten Mouse.
Please run after her!"

"I don't want to," said Cat.
"I have no need to frighten Mouse!"

"What a very bad cat you are!" cried Sparrow.
"I will tell Dog to chase you!"

Dog was resting in the corner of the barn.
"Please chase that naughty cat,"
said Sparrow to Dog.

"No!" said Dog. "I'm trying to sleep.
Go away, Sparrow. You're annoying me!"

"Well, *you* are annoying *me*!" shouted Sparrow.

Just then, Sparrow saw Flea jumping about.
"Flea!" said Sparrow.
"Please jump in Dog's ear and bite her."

So Flea jumped into Dog's ear
and bit her hard.

Now Dog could not sleep.
She cried out to Sparrow,
"Tell Flea to stop biting me and I will chase Cat."

"Flea, you can stop now," said Sparrow.

Soon, Dog began to run after Cat.

“Tell Dog to stop it!” cried Cat.
“I will frighten Mouse after all.”

“No!” cried Mouse.
“I will chew Old Pony’s tail after all!”

Just then, Crow flew into the barn.
Everyone stopped and looked at him.

"Sparrow!" said Crow. "What a big fuss you have made!
Let me show you what I put under my wing."

And he took out a tiny grain of rice.

"See!" said Crow. "You have made a big fuss
about a small thing!"

"Oh," said Sparrow, sadly. "You are right, Crow.
I was annoyed because you wouldn't show me
what you had found!
Now I have upset *everyone*.
I am sorry!"

"You can have the rice," Crow told Sparrow.

Sparrow was pleased.

"You are a good friend after all!" she said, happily.